The Mystic Side of
SCOTT

The Story of an Illustrated Mystic

DAVID KELLEY

MYSTIC

PAGE PUBLISHING, INC.
New York, NY

First originally published by Page Publishing, Inc. 2017

ISBN 978-1-64082-639-7 (Paperback)
ISBN 978-1-64082-640-3 (Digital)

Printed in the United States of America

Contents

Those who do not become aware of the mystic experience will not find eternal rest.

David S. Kelley, mystic

Before Birth

"Before our physical birth, there is a divine purpose for every soul that is born into this physical world. It matters not whether we are conceived out of wedlock or not nor that we are born in one part of the world or another as much as what we experience, learn, overcome, and how we deal with life and others. Every person born into this life comes with a mind ready to experience the world around it. Each newborn also comes into this world with abilities to be acted upon that will develop their faith and belief with a host of other factors coming into play. The question has been asked many times whether we have souls before we were born or that the soul is created at conception or at birth, but does it really matter anyway? No! This issue when pitted one against another only causes conflict and is useless and wastes time. Since there are millions of human beings born on earth, there are more influences at work than we can know and . . ."

"Okay, Scott, put away your writings. It's time to get ready to travel to Tulsa and acquire your new body through Lorene," stated Scott's guardian spirit.

"Damn, I don't like that name, Scott. I prefer that she call me David and not Scott," he replied.

"If you don't like it, then change it later on when you're ready," answered his guardian.

"Okay, okay, I'm ready," Scott responded.

Poof!

"Well, there goes Scott to his new mother. He should be ready this time to become a mystic and perform those spiritual duties [rites] for the Big Cheese," stated Scott's guardian.

"So I'm the Big Cheese!" God said.

"Oops, sorry, Your Eternalness!" answered the guardian to the Creator Eternal.

"Besides, Scott never could write or spell anyways," continued the spirit guardian.

"Always with the jokes, some say all that I've created is just another part of myself, yet all these individual parts of myself become one and knowing if those parts are of myself, I will discover that I'm the Eternal in every soul. Once this happens, then I become whole again," stated the Eternal Creator.

Each human soul then is destined to realize that upon its enlightenment that it was all along the Eternal fulfilling itself under prefect virtue as before its separation of itself.

The individual who becomes enlightened, the mystic, knows such perfect virtue of the Eternal that fulfills itself, and therefore each enlightened soul has self-realization that it is the Divine Eternal awakened all along. Since this is so, then every human born is part of everyone's Eternal Self yet to be realized once they awaken from their illusory dream of themselves.

Birth and the Young Years

So Scott leaves the spiritual side and enters the physical world, leaving his friends and spiritual guardian behind.

It was a summer's day, and a new baby boy is born unto the world with a full head of white hair, which is said by some to be the sign of an old soul about to become a mystic within his lifetime.

Scott naturally forgot his spiritual realm, and his physical mind developed until he remembered things and events at age three that happened to him physically.

"Look at all these things, and this person must be my mother," Scott thinks after Lorene told him who she was.

He took all these things for granted without forming any opinions or prejudice.

"My name is Scott," he was told and taught. As any child in the physical world, Scott viewed all things with an open mind and honest heart.

Scott comes to love and trust his mother and discovers that he has a younger brother named Preston to play with.

As the years passed, the two boys grew, with the same carefree heart and mind.

As the years passed, Scott had hard times, and childhood illnesses would have it. He found school interesting at first, but what troubled Scott was that some of his behaviors brought him physical punishment that hurt. Staying in his room, not playing with his friends or going outside the house caused him to feel sad and all alone.

Scott soon forgot these punishments, and as the years passed, he became aware of many things that one should not do, which meant that they were restrictive behaviors, which went against his free-spirited nature.

His free spirit caused many people to think that he had mental problems as he was always getting into trouble; conforming to such standards was hard enough for him to obey. Scott was told that he was intelligent and that he should know better than to get into trouble and straighten up. He just couldn't get the hang of school nor such education when the whole world was waiting for him to be explored and experienced.

Scott found himself drawing dinosaurs, inventing things, exploring the neighborhood, and just having fun playing.

When his family traveled, he went with them around the country, which relieved him of any responsibilities and demands from society. Scott enjoyed the freedom it gave him.

By traveling, Scott found that it rejuvenated his spirit, mind, and heart. These adventures kept him out of the reach of people who would take advantage of his honesty and goodness of heart.

Scott started running away from home and learned how to talk to strangers so he could obtain food, money, etc.

Trying different methods like hitchhiking, Scott found that these helped him in his travels, which assured him of such abilities to remain free and on the road.

In Scott's travels, he met many interesting souls, revealing their side of life, which they proved quite helpful. They were as honest as he was in spirit.

The old saying of "Don't talk to strangers" proved worthless and unwise to Scott in his travels for protection because he felt that he had a higher goal and purpose in life. Advice from others in his travels proved helpful in many ways.

Once Scott got the hang of how to present himself to the general public, the more he acquired in food, money, or whatever he needed and desired. Some people would say that Scott's lifestyle made him a tramp, no-account, con man, or a nonconformist.

Scott thought to himself, *What do they know?* and dismissed their words.

Later on, he began to wonder and question others' intentions about him and of life generally. As the years passed, Scott formed a mental image of a human figure of himself standing before a tree with different kinds of fruit hanging from its limbs.

When Scott would need answers to his questions or needed something, he would go to this tree and pick off that fruit and eat it, which in so doing would provide the solution for him.

As Scott reached his adulthood, he became more daring to where he would break into businesses at night to steal beer, cigarettes, and money. After a few of these burglaries, Scott's luck ran out, and he discovered what the judicial system meant and what a change of life in prison really means for everyone.

The saying that goes, "God works in mysterious ways," would prove for Scott to be his blessing in disguise.

In the ancient of times up to our present day, there have been born certain unorthodox individuals that are ready for the higher powers that be for the Eternal's essence to develop through them.

In Scott's case, the Divine's essence would work through him later on in his life. A man-child born unto this world of mystical origin is destined for a greater cause than mankind or himself.

Oh, mankind, how sure you are of your pride, intertwining the material world with your heart and soul, yet all your accomplishments are for naught because your souls are still unfulfilled unto the Absolute Eternal Consciousness for your eternal rest.

Prisons

Scott enjoyed his daring adventures and soon found himself abusing his liberties and discovered what it meant to be a burglar. The law of averages would soon catch up with him, and Scott found himself face to face at the point of the barrel of a policeman's gun. Scott was hauled off to jail, put before a judge, and sentenced to prison.

He spent a few years then released, but as fate would have it, Scott found himself in another prison in his early twenties. By this time, Scott began wondering about his life and what the *truth* really was about God.

One day, Scott prayed to God that the truth would be revealed to him of God. This prayer was prayed in earnest with an open heart and mind. Scott's answer to his prayers did not come to him that year or the year after that.

A few years later, while yet in another prison, Scott had just finished reading a religious book; he prayed in earnest again for God to reveal a vision as the ones he had read about to him. Without warning, Scott's consciousness was instantly merged with the Eternal Consciousness of God's (Absolute Consciousness). As suddenly as emergence took place, Scott found himself back in his own consciousness again. This happened so suddenly that it left him somewhat shocked and awe within his soul. Scott knew that his conscious awareness had been altered by the experience. Years later, he would learn that this altered state of consciousness is called mystic consciousness.

By such enlightenment, Scott experiences aftereffects of seeing a photograph of a man on a calendar talking to him yet not hearing what was said physically. Such mystic awareness is understood as total union with the Divine.

Scott later realized after studying what was written about the experience that this divine union was the truth, which was the answer to his prayers.

Scott was released from prison after his experience.

Little did Scott know that the Divine still had another plan for him, yet he would again find himself in another penitentiary to serve God's purpose.

Once again, Scott found himself within another prison in which he began studying many spiritual writings and books to find out what happened to him years earlier.

Going within himself, Scott experienced psychic visions, saw his spiritual guardian, and had prophetic dreams and visions. In such books on these subjects, Scott found that the meaning they offered didn't make sense nor were his fate and that another Divine experience was in store for him.

Fate was in the wind for Scott, for his research led him to seek an organization of psychic readings, and once he was released from prison again, he set out upon his quest to find what purpose and other truths that might be in store for him.

Scott headed off to this spiritual center he had read about. Once he arrived, he entered the building's library section and randomly thumbed through some of the psychic volumes of readings. As fate would have it, Scott came across another answer, which read, "The answers are found in our subconscious mind." After reading this message, Scott felt as if an empty void within him had been filled.

What Scott didn't know was that he was about to be introduced to the means that would open the door between the physical realm and the spiritual world that would allow one to perform sacrifices for the Almighty to benefit mankind. It is a matter between God and the servant regardless of what is written and accepted from any other religion, faith, or belief of any society. Christ, Buddha, Lao Tzu, Siddhartha, and others all had their spiritual rituals, and Scott would soon experience his with the Eternal Creator (God).

The Eternal Divine has its own nature not of man's—such receptive individuals as Christ, Buddha, and Lao Tzu, who have cast aside all others and seek for themselves this truth of the Absolute. Scott was one of these individuals.

The Nonconformist

Some individuals such as Scott were born into this world as a non-conformist. Scott felt that he did not belong to any place on earth nor did he fit in with any group as so many others did. Most people he knew and met had steady jobs, married, had children, or belonged to some lifestyle. They had a bond in some way to this physical world, yet Scott felt out of place and had a wanderlust.

Some nonconformists are bound by the Divine as outcasts from society and do not have a resting place on earth to call home. At every turn in life, these nonconformists are dissatisfied with the world of mankind because the earth is not really their home or resting place of body, mind, and soul, as others seem to be and hold firmly onto.

Society considers nonconformists as having personality disorders while others would take the opportunity to assault them, yet others would try to advise them not to do this or that because it is not good for them.

Christ, Buddha, Lao Tzu, Nichiren Shoshu, and others were nonconformists to the moral majority and standards of mankind's world. Even such moral societies are useless for the Eternal Divine's essence, and such enlightened nonconformists are advanced elder brethren of all of mankind in human evolution that can become God (Absolute).

Such enlightened nonconformists break away from such morals and standards of the common faith and belief that are assumed to be the only truths.

Some religious persons who have experienced this Divine Presence (the Mystic Experience) have considered it secondary to their religions and have misplaced it.

Scott came to accept that he also was a spiritual brother with the enlightened ones as Christ, Buddha, and Lao Tzu and not religious. As we shall shortly find out, Scott is about to find the means to use the blessings of the divine primal virtue from the good primal guardians begotten from the Absolute (Tao).

Spiritual Seed Planted

Upon leaving the spiritual center and library, Scott camped out on the beach and worked at a few odd jobs. He met another young man, whom he moved in with, and since they both enjoyed beer and small parties, things worked out between the two.

Scott noticed that there was an oriental scroll encased in an oriental shrine with foreign writings on the scroll in the living room of his roommate's apartment. Inquiring as to what the scroll was, Scott was informed that it fulfilled one's desired wishes and that one could obtain eternal happiness.

Scott was invited to attend one of the weekly chant meetings that afternoon.

When he arrived at the home where the meeting was held, Scott was introduced to many people and found another scroll and shrine. Scott was shown how to chant, pronouncing the strange words from a chant booklet. As the chanting progressed, an aura of unity developed as one voice within the room.

This chanting lasted an hour, and when it was finished, Scott was informed that he could obtain one of these scrolls for a small fee, so with the last of the cash Scott had, he gave the money to one of the leaders of the meeting, leaving his name with them.

As the days passed, Scott attended more of these meetings and found that a few of his desires were fulfilled, but this seemed as if it was only for one's personal selfish ends.

Finally, the day came for Scott to obtain his scroll, so he went with a few friends to a large meeting hall. He found a place on the floor to sit and chanted for an hour until a priest came out in front before another scroll and began calling names of each person in the room to hand them their scrolls.

Scott's name was called, and he got up, walked to the priest, knelt down, and was handed his scroll.

The moment that the scroll touched Scott's open hands, he could feel a sense that a spiritual seed had been planted within himself just above his physical heart. This spot is the spiritual pouch of the human body's soul.

After the meeting, Scott left with the people he had come with and went to where he was staying. He felt that everything was in order within him, so he didn't worry about it.

Some days later, Scott packed his belongings and left the area. A few days later, he found a job and place to stay, and he built his own shrine and chanted for a few days.

This arrangement did not last long, so Scott packed up and headed west. Sometime later, he left his pack with his scroll in it with a young couple, and the next morning, he found out that they had left town with his belongings and scroll.

Later on, Scott would find out that his scroll had already served its purpose for the spiritual guardian's plans for him as being the means for the planting of the spiritual seed.

Planting, sewing, and harvesting of such spiritual virtue for all of mankind through such individual mystic comes in many forms and events.

The Mystic Dreams

Around this time in Scott's life, while in his late twenties, there appeared to him many spiritual dreams.

The first symbolic dream was of Satan (the Devil) in Christianity, popping up from behind a wooden log, asking him who he believed in, Satan or Jesus.

Scott answered Jesus, then the dream ended. In another dream, Scott was walking toward Jesus (Christ). His back was turned toward Scott, and Christ called Scott by his spiritual name, David.

Jesus stated, "David, I want you to go out unto the world and invite rich, poor, bond, free, all to come to my supper."

Behind Christ was a table with white linen laid over it.

Scott answered Jesus, saying, "Yes, master."

After these words were spoken, Scott turned to his right and walked toward a door frame standing by itself. He walked through it. The dream ended at this point.

To most spiritually inclined people, this could be a calling to become a Christian minister to serve Jesus. Scott felt that these dreams were spiritual in nature but that there were too many Christian organizations, and from his many other spiritual experiences, it meant something else later on in his life.

It would be a hard thing to get past the fear of having evil take you to hell if one did not follow and believe in Jesus in this religion. In the Christian religions, they all tell you that you have to have blind faith in their words and ways, because as the Bible states, there is no other way to be saved.

Scott thought to himself, *I wonder if they can take their Bibles with them to heaven when they pass on. No, I don't think so. It appears that any kind of religion, belief, or faith of mankind does not fit me.*

In another dream, Scott and another woman (Scott's subconscious mind) were sitting in a room (of his mind), and as they talked, they were interrupted. A door opened, and in the doorway stood a dark (black) figure that Scott knew instantly as his physical death (passing). The dream ended, yet in the years to come, he again dreamed of death paying him a visit.

Though Scott had many dreams, there was one that let him know what the Divine's essence was to be and preparing him for such service.

This dream is as follows:

Scott found himself sitting on a bench, dressed in an oriental monk's robe with his head shaven. Next to him sat his spiritual master teacher to his left. Scott's master told him that it was time to perform his spiritual rites of service. As Scott was about to get up and leave the bench, he looked up to his left over a stone wall at the sky, and he had another mystic experience shown to him. It was like the first one he had many years ago of the Eternal Consciousness of the Absolute.

After this experience ended, Scott walked to a small shrine in front of him that was off to the left side of a larger shrine, and he performed what was expected of him correctly. Once finished, Scott turned around to his right and headed back toward the bench were he had come from.

As he did so, he passed an old oriental man that Scott knew as Lao Tzu. The old man smiled at Scott, acknowledging that he was well pleased with him.

When Scott returned to his bench and sat down, he found that his master teacher had vanished and that he was with shaven head anew.

His robe meant something important now. Scott looked at his left hand and arm to find that a mystical dragon of the Orient was tattooed on him there.

The dragon's tail and back legs were on his forearm while the main body and front legs were wrapped around his arm. Its head ended up on his left shoulder blade facing to Scott's right of red and blue. At this point, the spiritual dream ended.

Thou this dream was symbolic, Scott did perform similar rituals later on spiritually. At a later date in the physical manifestation of Scott's life, these rites did happen, and an understanding of Lao Tzu's Tao Te Ching developed.

Down through history, some individuals are born with the natural ability to do service unto the Eternal Divine from any part of the world to benefit mankind. To doubt this should show one has not faced the Divine Eternal and may indeed be blind and lost to this truth. To demand everyone else to join in one religious belief is a prejudice, but the mystic with the divine rites needs not the world's religions. Another time, Scott was blessed by and healed by religious members of a spiritual/mental affliction.

The Eternal Tree

As time passed, Scott found himself in another prison, and this time, he wanted to get out of that situation but finding that he had to complete the sentence of the judgment against him. Scott remembered his chanting and sent for the little chant booklet.

In the meantime, while waiting to receive it, Scott meditated, which seemed to open the door to the demon world that entered him. These negative spirits Scott felt as if they were attacking to control his soul or drive him mad.

Scott's age was thirty-three years at this time he experience them, it is believed. Each day, more demons would enter him, yet he had to solve this problem.

Scott started chanting some of the words he knew, but this didn't work until he made up his mind and demanded of the Divine that these demons leave him, and he used his force of spiritual will in prayer. Then as suddenly as they entered him, they all left him.

A few weeks later, Scott received his chant booklet and set about putting forth his desire to chant his way out of prison. As it turned out, a totally different experience happened to him.

One night, as Scott lay on his bed, he was taken by the Eternal Divine again, but instead of the Eternal Divine going away, Scott's conscious awareness was cast into a total Dark Black Veil that divided him from the Eternal Light and the spiritual world of souls. At that same moment, Scott's soul asked the Eternal if he could perform a service after there appeared three pinholes through this Dark Black Veil (void).

Then after the request was asked, two of the holes closed to Scott's right and middle, but the eternal light remained open to his left. This eternal presence was the same as the other ones Scott knew, and it approved and consented to his desire and question of his request. The Eternal Divine's presence ended, and this was a further communication between man's soul and the Divine Eternal Absolute. Within a few days, Scott could feel a burning sensation within his spine from top to bottom.

Scott began to wonder if he was dying or just what was happening to him. He finally gave up fighting this spiritual fire and prayed again to his God (the Eternal), putting total trust in it for whatever lay ahead for him. Scott chanted every day when he received his chant booklet, and still, this Test by Spiritual Fire was upon him. He slept, ate, went about his daily life under this test for many weeks.

Scott thought of another book he used as a tool called *I Ching: Book of Change*. To use it, he would thumb through it, pointing to whichever sentence his finger would stop on. He would obtain an answer, which was a way of informing him, done by his Guardian Spirit, what was happening.

Scott obtained this book again and used it in these matters for answers.

One day, Scott found that the staining emotions of guilt, shame, and all manners of adultism was removed up off his soul. Becoming clean of soul again, he could see clearly as when he was a child, void of any prejudice, stain, or adulteration (forgiveness of sin). This is the concept of being born again of spirit as Jesus talked about.

One night, while Scott was asleep, he felt his soul being stung by something that hurt and caused great pain of his soul. As he fell back asleep, he was stung a second time, but now he saw what stung him, which was a little demon having the shape of a bee with a human face with two stingers on it. One of the stingers was for a tail, and the other one for its nose.

As this demon flew away from Scott, it stated, "I got you again." Once Scott could see such demons face to face with his spiritual eye, then such negative (evil) ones would stop bothering him.

Another time, when Scott was trying to go to sleep, he felt his will to live slipping away from him. It got to the point where Scott believed that he was at death's door, so he forced himself to fight back and will himself mentally to live.

Again, this happened to his will, and again, he willed his will to live to come back to him, and it remained this time. Scott found that his will came back stronger than ever.

He remembered an old saying that stated, "Before we can influence and benefit others, we must first master ourselves."

Some days later, Scott had a vision of a spiritual fruit appearing. Its stem grew and developed purple fruits from thin air. There appeared some five to six of these fruits, and the last fruit was the largest of them all.

Another time, Scott saw heat vapors all around him as if of desert heat waves. This was the effects of the test by spiritual fire of purification.

Another time, as he lay upon his bed, awake, he noticed that it felt as if he was like a tree with its roots starting to grow in his legs, its branches sprouting through his arms. As it grew, it felt to him as a young spiritual tree developing to maturity. Some say, "Lotus." This was the spiritual seed that was planted within him years ago.

One could say that this is the Tree of Life. This growth is the birth and growing pains of the spiritual tree to produce spiritual fruits of divine virtue and grace. This was so painful that after it stopped, it took Scott a few days to get back to somewhat being normal physically.

As Scott was contemplating these experiences, he saw a vision of an elderly woman with a string of pearls around her neck. She was looking at him as if to say that she was there to protect and nurture him. This is the primal mother of mystics. She joined his rites then for that purpose of primal virtue.

A few days later, Scott felt a great fear and trembling in stark terror welling up within him. He was screaming at the top of his whole being within his soul, but his screaming did not come through to his physical voice.

Scott thought he was near his protector in spirit. It was reassuring to him at that time, yet he was all alone. He understood that he was standing before his soul's creator that could destroy it. His soul was being judged on the spiritual level standing naked and hiding nothing. When this experience was over, Scott was very relieved!

A few days later, as he was sitting cross-legged on his bed, he felt as if from the top of his head, a spiritual center of the human body, a warm light was shining upon him, but not a light in the physical sense. Scott couldn't understand this while this was happening; he thumbed through his *I Ching* and pointed to a passage that stated, "The superior man distributes his virtue while he accumulates it, or he will have a violent collapse."

This made sense to him, and the meaning of this warm light was spiritual virtue from the Divine. Scott spoke up and stated, "I give virtue to," and started naming persons, countries (nations), others just being born and others just dying, etc. What was on Scott's mind at the time was the mass number of human souls in the world and not the government's ideology such as democracy, socialism, communism, nor any form of religion, faith, or belief.

In some cases, when trying to give out virtue, none was given out. This is to be understood as one sacrificing all, even one's very soul, to the Creator before such Divine Virtue can be brought unto mankind's souls of the world to bless them. These are the Divine's aim and plan for us. After this experience had ended, Scott was thankful that it had happened.

Some days later, Scott received two visions. One was of him walking to his freedom—that is he saw himself walking out of the darkness from a building into the suburbs. The second vision was showing him money numbers as the amount of money he would receive in the future.

When these two visions had been revealed to Scott, he sensed that the elderly spiritual lady in his earlier vision was nurturing him in spirit and unto his soul back to well-being. She is the Great Mother of such enlightened men of the world stated by Lao Tzu.

Scott saw within his mind as if he was a sage sitting upon a royal throne coming unto authority. When viewing himself in a mirror, Scott saw the anger welling up within him, and yet he was in control of it. Scott knew that the time had come to where such spiritual experiences were coming to their conclusion. That now was the time for total nourishing and healing by the Great Mother of mystic souls to his spiritual well-being of Primal Mother's sons.

Exploring the inward substance of his physical mind, Scott found it as when one would hold up thin human skin to a light and see all the blood veins and other parts with some dim light. He saw himself before the Great Void, or Great Gulf, that divides mankind from the spiritual. Scott found that his subconscious mind was trying to draw his conscious awakened state to it. At the max of this experience of this drawing inward, there was a release of this grip of him.

After the second time this happened, Scott had to willfully control and force it back to its servant position or else he would be at its mercy. Things once again settled back down in harmony and balance.

The old saying, "If you're not a master carpenter you will only get hurt," also implies that if you're not born to experience and master these inward dealings, you only hurt yourself.

One's pureness of heart and soul in the true essences of being is the tool for the Eternal Divine's essence as a man-child for humanity within these rites!

To marry upon earth, one merges in vows and devotion. Marrying in mystic spiritual rites merges one in divine union with the Absolute!

The Virtue Blessing

Scott's guardian spirit stated to another spirit, "Well, Scott really suffered, yet he sure had the right heart for all that virtue from the Eternal."

"Yes, he has," replied the other spirit, "and the other spirits and souls are well pleased with him because of all that Scott gives out. The Eternal is bound now to up hold and honor it".

"Why do you suppose the Eternal Divine choose Scott and give him consent to do these sacred sacrifices?" asked the other spirit.

Scott's guardian answered, saying, "Who knows, I guess the Divine's begotten wanted to use someone who was ready to have eternal revelation in the true mystic sense and wouldn't have any religion, faith, or belief get in the way, and Scott fit the bill."

"Most people would think that a criminal like Scott would be a liar about these experiences because he is not a religious person. Besides, he uses tobacco and drinks beer when he's on the streets," stated the other spirit to the guardian.

"Oh, that's just one of those physical things, but the Eternal doesn't care about that its one's soul being pure that counts," answered the guardian.

"What about all that virtue from the Eternal Scott gave out?" asked the spirit.

The guardian answered the other spirit, saying, "Well, since all that virtue of spiritualness Scott gave out was to bless the souls on earth still living within their human bodies and will be honored spiritually."

"Look at Scott now. He hasn't got a clue, does he?" stated the spirit.

"Scott will come to understand later," answered the guardian.

The guardian continued, "You see, some individuals like Scott come to understand that prison can become like a monastery or temple. Sometimes it is more effective to be in such a place for the Divine's essence. Spiritual virtue is of the soul in suffering greatly to bless others. Scott is a soul that fits that bill and is the mediator between man and God, the sacrificed soul upon the cross, the chosen of pure soul and heart, tested by spiritual fire. The Christ, Buddha, Lao Tzu, Siddhartha, and the Mystic fit the Divine (Tao, God) and guardians goodness and virtue. Mankind left unto themselves without a spiritual tie-in to the Divine Eternal, nor a mediator tends to take another step toward barbarous. Their souls then would not have a saving grace on the spiritual side after they pass from this physical realm, and they would find no progressive step to the Eternal Divine mergence past the Dark Black Veil of Ignorance. The soul is also one's conscious awareness made known to itself and can realize that it is also the Absolute consciousness in enlightenment, the eternal self ever present."

The Visions

"Guardian spirit, what about all those visions Scott had that was revealed to him?" asked the other spirit.

"First, you have to understand what a vision is for one person and the term *vision* to another. Some people see visions as in one's imagination of physical thoughts only without anything real behind them. They have not become aware of spiritual revelation of the supernatural or divine nature. Scott's visions are prophetic, but they are of the Eternal as well. Some of Scott's visions are symbolic though," answered the guardian.

"How can one tell how true visions are and imaginary ones?" asked the spirit.

The guardian replied, "Real visions are revealed to someone in a sudden flash of insight from the spiritual side and are shocking to one's soul in reality. It's like being in a dimly lit room and suddenly the door opens and shines bright sunlight in your eyes and then the door is suddenly closed again. It leaves a lasting impression upon one's consciousness and soul. The mystic experience is a vision of the highest order of conscious awareness of reality that has one merge with the Eternal Divine's state of being in pure consciousness. Anyone who has this experience has obtained the final goal of mankind and has become the Absolute Perfect."

"What do you mean Absolute Perfect?" asked the spirit.

The guardian stated, "Absolute Perfect means utterly complete and faultless as the Eternal Divine, God, and once obtained, that soul has become complete and pure to perfection. No moral law, religion, society of any kind, or any type of civilization. Not even the spiritual realm can make one Absolute Perfect, only the Divine itself. It's between the Divine Eternal and that soul only that counts! Jesus, Buddha, Lao Tzu, Nichiren, Siddhartha, and the mystics are the ones who come unto God and not by a go-between. Not by Jesus, Buddha, Lao Tzu, Nichiren, nor Siddhartha, but by oneself only to the Eternal Divine, Absolute. Most souls of mankind do not know the Absolute Perfect because if known or realized, they would find eternal rest at the end of their lives on earth and be merged in Absolute Perfect Consciousness. This would put an end to their separateness, suffering, individuality, darkness, ignorance, and all manner of unenlightenment. This is the highest state of mankind."

The House of Three Flames

Eventually, Scott was released from prison after his spiritual revelations with the Eternal and once again wandered around the country. Scott thought, *Things seem to be in the form of the Three Eternal Lights I saw when I obtained the Eternal's consent to perform those sacrifices (rite). I think that the world is of three-in-one dimension we live within.*

Sometime later, Scott sat down and began writing to try to make sense of the world and of what he had studied and experienced. He wrote a story and entitles it *The House of Three Flames.*

Scott wrote the following:

A young man came upon an odd-shaped building in a clearing in the forest. The building was in the shape of one of those in the Orient with up-turned corners of the roof. Above each comer of the roof was a spiritual living flame, but the material of the building did not fuel these flames the spirit did. There was a double door but no windows to be seen.

He walked through the doors and saw a large room, which was the only room in the building. On the right wall were large jars on shelves, which in each jar had a strange creature in it. The young man walked further into the room yet noticed it was empty of all other things except a back door. Approaching the wall of jars, he reached out to touch one of them and heard a voice from behind him speak saying, "I wouldn't touch any of those jars if I were you."

The young man turned around and saw an ancient-looking man sitting on a bench that had materialized across the room on the far wall.

The young man walked up to the ancient one and asked, "Why shouldn't I touch them?"

"Sit down next to me, and I will explain," the old man told him.

The young man sat down and listened.

"You see, young man, those jars belong to three realms of the physical, mental, and spiritual realizations. If you touch any of those jars, this is the same as agreeing to allow yourself to enter that creature's realm, which causes the absorption of your body, mind, and soul into that creature's world and its reality. Once you enter their world, it's almost impossible to leave it again because their reality becomes your reality. Their realities also come with its own consequences and rewards, whether we like them or not. It's the principle of cause and effect," the ancient one continued.

"Then why are these jars in the first place in this strange house?" asked the young man.

The old one replied, "These jars are here to hold them in control. They act as a focus point for the person that is on their quest to become enlightened to the mystic experience."

"Then what and why the house then?" asked the young man.

"This house is the human conscious mind where the soul is awake to see if any realities are to be experienced of the jars or if that person has me appears to them here as a guide if they listen to one such as I am or not," stated the old one.

"Then if one touches one of the jars, they lose their way to finding their enlightenment because none of these jars can offer it to them," explained the young man.

The ancient one answered him, saying, "Now you're beginning to understand the path along the way when one is on their quest. Once someone has entered the realm of these creatures, there is a way back out of that reality. It is like a mirror in which when one looks into the mirror, they will dimly see this house again. Once they desire to enter this house, it becomes much harder because the creatures' world has stained their souls' sight so they can't see clearly. Anyone in those realities must use their soul and the spiritual guardians to obtain their help to cross back over into this house where one like me will be waiting. Once they have reentered this room, they will either stay or take the path onwards out this back door. They can leave by the double doors and go back to where they started from."

The young man asked the old one, "What of the three living flames I saw before I entered this house?"

"These three living flames are the three dimensions created and held by the Eternal. It knows all minds, hearts, and souls of all who are found in this house. It also knows the creatures' minds, hearts, and souls, as well as mine," answered the ancient one.

The young man pondered upon these things and then asked the old man, "Then who and why are you here?"

"I'm your guardian and guide when you entered this atmosphere and your quest of this house. Your quest is one who desires to discover the real truth of one's Absolute Eternal Self without getting sidetracked by the jars. You have rejected all the jars and do not wish to return from once you came.

"The jars and this building show one that all other realities are only side effects along the way on their quest to their enlightenment. Guardians such as I are here to help souls. To human beings, we are our own reality to be guides for others such as yourself when desired and/or needed.

"When people use religious prayers to ask for help from their god or savior, such as Jesus or Buddha, they do not see or know that it is their spiritual guardians that take on that figure of the one who is believed in that faith to justify to that person's faith. Guardians are here to help and guide the human soul through this house to eternal enlightenment of the mystic experience. This house also is when one is in pristine simplicity without being adulterated or proud.

"The Eternal's essence is of two kinds of revelations that human soul's experience. The first is experiencing the mystic awakening of the Eternal Absolute, and the second is experiencing the spiritual sacrifices of offering one's soul for supreme purification, suffering, and divine virtue for mankind's soul. In either case, that person enters the Cave of the Enlightened. This quest is to discover the truth of God (the Eternal Divine).

"Mankind has a need to give names to the Eternal, and no matter what name is given, it seems that names cannot describe what God is supposed to be called or really is. The Eternal has been called by many names, such as God, Tao, Divine, Absolute, Eternal,

Supreme, Deity, Mystic, Heavenly Father, etc. These names placed upon the Ultimate have an effect with religions or faiths. Somehow it is supposed to separate their God from all the others to make theirs more important than the rest. Only individuals such as you, young man, have set all that aside and seek their personal experience of the Eternal that is the truth.

"Follow me, young man, and I will guide you to the Void of the Great Cave of the Enlightened, the Hermit's Cave to the Eternal," stated the old one to the young one.

So the young man followed the ancient one out the back door of the House of Three Flames and followed him on the path toward the cave.

"Explain how the cave works," asked the following young man.

"The cave is that state of mind where one's conscious awareness enters when one has cast off and rejected all else, even life itself, to discover the truth of the Eternal (the mystic experience). That becomes the conviction of their soul of the Divine Absolute. At that moment, the Eternal will reveal itself to that person because that person is ready to receive it. This is the final stage of mankind," explained the guardian (the ancient one) to the young man.

Scott put away his writings and went upon his way. His future now turns toward new insights and understandings of the human character, his elder years, and many concepts.

Visions Fulfilled

"So what of Scott and his future?" asked the spirit to Scott's guardian.

"Now that Scott is fifty-seven years old at this moment, he has finally learned to stay out of prison because he no longer needs such institutions as ministries. Scott's camping out on the streets and writing about his spiritual experiences of his past. He's found that he no longer needs to try to fit into any advanced society where others seem to fit in with as their reality. Scott has become in tuned and in harmony with nature in pristine simplicity," stated the guardian.

"But Scott listens to his radio and travels to town to buy the things he needs," explained the spirit.

"Though Scott lives in the woods, he still needs items and enjoys talking to others. Scott is waiting for his last two visions to materialize," answered the guardian.

"After Scott's visions materialize, then what does he do?" asked the spirit.

Scott's guardian replied, "Scott will spend a short time at a motel in a small town so he can obtain some items he needs for his travels to a foreign land. He always wanted to travel to some small island in the Pacific and live in a small village. Scott studied ancient philosophies of living a 'pristine simplicity' way of life so this should help him. The Tao Te Ching by Lao Tzu has such philosophies in his writings as the Pacific Islanders use."

"Scott could buy a house or invest in stocks and bonds with the money he gets from his visions," stated the spirit.

"Scott would have never been satisfied remaining in his country with its philosophies, morals, laws, and a host of other things. Scott discovered that the modern world with its advancements are in conflict with his unity of the Eternal, which society never did have a hold on him anyway. The Eternal Almighty knows Scott, and the guardians did provide him those two visions, and these will help him with the means to travel overseas for another primal aim. The present world has started its Great Tribulation, and Scott no longer is influenced by any of it. He knows that the world is no longer his place because Scott is a part of the Eternal in spirit," answered the guardian.

"Then what else is there left for Scott to do in his country before he leaves?" asked the spirit.

"If possible, he will try to visit his mother for a short time then leave the country. If she is not alive, then he could visit her grave, etc.," replied the guardian.

"So after that, then what?" inquired the spirit.

"Scott will leave his country, never to return again, and live out the rest of his life in some village to help them and teach his philosophies as the Tao Te Ching, *I Ching*, and others have fun in the sun with the villagers and become one of them," answered the guardian.

"Is there a chance that Scott could die and pass on before his visions materialize?" asked the spirit.

"Not until Scott's visions have come to fruition and not until his seventy-second year is upon him of his earlier visions. The Eternal has sealed his fate," answered the guardian.

Scott's age at his death was revealed to him long ago in his chanting, age seventy-two years old upon his passing.

Some enlightened individuals have many visions of divine revelations. This is natural to such persons for the Absolute to enlarge itself toward its once held being to the Utmost as it once was.

The Foreign Village

The jetliner landed on the islands of Tr in the Micronesians in the Pacific Ocean. Scott walked down the ramp and into the customs office as did other passengers. Scott waited in line and when it was his turn to approach the desk, the officer asked him, "How long are you planning on staying on our islands?"

"As long as possible. I'm a mystic philosopher of the Universal Life Church, and I hope to stay here and study the village people, live amongst them to write about their lives," explained Scott.

Scott showed him his ID and paid for a permit for a year, passed his onward airline ticket to him as well. He was given his papers back with a stamped card and other documents when he was finished and walked out the front door.

There were island people in town when he arrived, and he asked one of them where he could find someone to take him to some of the islands within the area. He was taken to an islander, and Scott explained what he wanted and that he would need the man's services in a few days. The man agreed to meet him at the hotel where Scott would be staying.

Scott left carrying his bags and a box of books to the hotel and rented a room for a few days. When he got to his room, he put his belongings on the bed and went to the nearest cafe to eat. After his meal, he headed to the hotel room to rest.

When he had closed the door to his room, he opened his bag and took out a fifth of rum, poured himself a glass, and sipped on it. Scott lit a cigarette, walked to the window, and took in the view.

The town, sky, ocean, and view were just like he had seen in the travel manuals. He felt tired from his long trip, so he went to the bed, sat down, putting the glass down on the end table. Scott showered, came out putting his belongings on the floor, and lay on the bed naked to fully dry off. Before he knew it, he was asleep.

The next morning, he got dressed, lit another cigarette, and took another drink from the glass of rum. He headed out the door, and leaving the hotel, he headed for the cafe to have breakfast.

After his morning meal, he walked down the street to shop for suitable clothes for island life. Scott noticed that everywhere he went the island people were most friendly and greeted him most politely as he passed them. He took in the view of the town and its surroundings.

After his rent ran out and he was getting ready to leave the hotel, his guide appeared at the door, which Scott let him in. Scott explained that he wanted to be taken to another island called Wiui.

After arriving on this island by boat and walking on shore, Scott was taken to a small store by his guide. Meeting the store owner, Scott bought a few things. Paying his guide, Scott met other villagers, and since he was a new stranger, they took him to their village.

The village was made up of huts with palms and wood open-air buildings for cooling, which Scott guessed twenty in number.

The whole village came out to meet him, and he was taken to the chief and his wife to meet. To the island people, this new stranger meant that it was a celebration, which the whole community turned out. This was a time to make this new visitor a member of the village family. A mild alcoholic beverage was made and served to Scott, the chief, and everyone else.

Some of the villagers danced, and after some small talk, Scott explained that he wanted to live among them, to write about them, that he had hopes of explaining his philosophies as a storyteller to anyone who would be interested in learning. Scott was taken to a hut to stay for a while.

As Scott was settling down for the night, a native woman came into the hut and lay down beside him. Scott didn't know what to make of this, so he went to sleep.

The next morning, when he awakened, he found that the woman was gone. As he was getting ready for the day, another woman came in and led him outside to where other villagers were sitting, and the morning meal was served and eaten.

After eating, Scott questioned some of the group about many things on how he wanted to be their teacher, yet the villagers wanted to know all about him also.

As it worked out after the first few days, he made arrangements with the authorities to stay on the island for another year. As the days past he became their village educator, writer, philosopher, and storyteller.

Scott started his journals on the native people and went around talking to everyone to learn of their customs, ideas, and philosophize.

He did finally meet and agree to have a woman sleep with him, and since the children's curiosity got the best of them, Scott made friends with them easily, and they were into everything, yet they proved helpful. Scott married the woman who lived with him, and he was granted citizenship.

In the meantime, Scott's writings were sent off to the publishers, and they wanted him to sign papers for an agreement to publish them. He agreed, and after some months, Scott was sent a small amount of money into his bank account.

Since it didn't take much money to live on the island, Scott used most of his bank account to help the villagers with their needs. Other sources Scott knew of proved helpful also that came through, and all was peaceful and calm with him, yet he still had the sense that he really didn't belong to any place on earth nor with these people also.

After a few months, his wife became pregnant, and the day of their child's birth, he found that he had a daughter. As the years passed, Scott's legs, back, and eyes were failing him, so he instructed his wife, daughter, and a few others on his teaching and journals for safekeeping.

One day, other villagers came from a far off island to see Scott to hear what he had to say. Scott knew that he only had a few years left because by now he was in his late sixties.

Since it had been revealed to him many years ago that he would be seventy-two years old when he would die, he traveled and visited other villages on other islands. Scott finally grew too old to continue traveling, so he returned to his village for the rest of his life.

As the days passed, he left word with the villagers that when he died, his body be taken out to sea and fed to the sharks so that his body would not be made a thing for a grave nor to be shipped back to civilization.

As the end came, Scott waited for death to take him so he could unite and rest eternally within the Divine Absolute Self.

Scott thought of all the things in his life and how he found his joy with the villagers.

The Passing

As the days passed, Scott found himself sensing as if his time to pass from the world and unite with the Eternal was soon to be upon him. He called the villagers and his family together and spoke unto them saying, "My time will soon be upon me, and I will pass on to join the Eternal. All these years I've been with you have brought me much joy and fulfillment. All of you, I've tried to bring knowledge of the philosophies of the enlightened men of the world, and I love you all. All of you are living the pristine way of life that matters and what is written about by those ancient mystics. Now that I've fulfilled my life, I turn all my writings and books over to my wife for safekeeping until the day when the world changes and becomes peaceful again. I bless all of you and hope that you have understood what I've been teaching you."

After Scott had finished speaking, the villagers left him and went about their daily activities.

That night, Scott felt the presence of his guardian spirit though he could not see him.

"Well, there's old Scott about to make his transition from the physical to unite with the Eternal," stated Scott's guardian to the other spirit.

As Scott slept that night, the transformation took place, and Scott's body was all that was left on earth.

"Now what are you going to do?" asked the spirit to the guardian.

"I've been assigned to help another soul," replied the guardian.

The villagers held true to Scott's wishes and took his body to the open ocean and put it into the sea. The sharks arrived and consumed it.

Scott's wife held true to her word also and kept his teachings. She continued educating the children and villagers until she became too old to continue.

Scott's daughter kept her father's materials to carry on.

Scott truly and finally merged with the Omniscient Eternal as every mystic has for eons and eons.

Mystics, such as Scott, for thousands of years from their births until their deaths, have all known this same Divine Eternal. As in Scott's case and so in all the others, they are the forerunner of all souls on earth to obtain the highest state of man, and so they are the elders, advanced of the ones left that are unaware of this state of consciousness. This is the great mergence of eternal cosmic law, which all souls must in one way or another come to eternal rest within sooner or later as the nature and character of the Absolute.

The Discussion

"So what's this all about that Scott and others of his kind make so much about their experiences in this so-called enlightenment?" asked the spirit.

"Well, the whole world of mankind holds each their own individual consciousness in and with their physical bodies and minds so that each soul is separate from each other and from the eternal divine. This allows each person the opportunity to have the will to step outside society's conformity and not be ruled by it as a robot, slave, or conformist to whatever is considered the way of man-made creations or of spirits. If it was so that each person must conform to society's standards, morals, laws, and beliefs, then mankind would be dependent upon whatever their leaders or authorities would order or say. There would not be any advancement into many of such mystic philosophies that reveal the truths about mankind, the soul, and the Eternal.

"Since mankind has freewill in independent thinking, they are able to ponder upon and develop themselves mentally and spiritually by choice of one's freewill. Most human beings that have lived on earth have fallen prey to either believing or not believing in another's faith, and those believers have some form of inward sense that their belief is the right faith or religion to their salvation.

"This is their individual makeup, and each person's consciousness is not known to another person normally. Fortunately for this, it allows each individual to have their own insights. Each person's own character allows them to accept or reject whatever belief, faith, or experiences, of others.

"Human minds are made up of personal experiences. Their quest in seeking insights to confirm to their conscious mind is when they are ready to discover the truths, and then they will be fulfilled within their souls. Some individuals reject beliefs, religions, books, organizations, and insights of the world and step outside all these because they are man's creations and are not Eternal ones or spiritual insights.

"By divine revelation, the mystic has the veil of ignorance lifted off their minds, then they discover eternal realities and other insights until they find what fits within their soul's fulfillment. People are able to change their held opinions and beliefs after the veil is lifted up off their soul's awareness as reality.

"*Homo sapiens* (humans) are made up of three parts: (1) a physical body, (2) mental and subconscious awareness of the mind, and (3) a spiritual and super consciousness (soul). The human physical body has needs and functions like all animals. It needs to eat, sleep, drink water, reproduce, and get rid of waste, and it needs warmth.

"The mental part of the human has functions of conscious awareness, emotions, thinking, and reasoning. This has the company of the subconscious mind with dreams, psychic awareness, and contemplates upon things for the conscious awaken and sleep states.

"The subconscious (unconscious) mind being connected to the conscious mind keeps the heart beating and other such functions because of one's life force (soul).

"The spiritual (super conscious) mind is the seat of the soul and, through the subconscious to the conscious mind, allows that person to perceive other dimensions known as the spiritual realm. With awareness of the spiritual realm, one has the ability to become aware of spirits, souls, and forces that are negative or positive to that person. The soul is that part of the human spirit that is immortal, which is a part of the Eternal Divine (God, Jesus, Buddha, and others). The spirit and soul of every human are not the same because the individual who has had the mystic experience with the Eternal Divine has had their souls awake to it. Souls that have not had this mystic awareness are awake but still asleep in ignorance of the Divine.

"Some would argue that the soul and spirit are the same and cannot become aware of the Eternal because they are separate and limited from the Immortal Creator. The mystic or enlightened ones do not accept the notion of the philosophy of separation between their soul and the Divine, God, Absolute. Once a person has experienced the Eternal Divine, they become that Eternal Divine, the one and the same within their soul's consciousness.

"Once this experience is realized within one's conscious awareness, all manner of the concepts of heaven, hell, religion, or what have you are proven not to be the case but man-made and spiritual not mystic.

"All then is cast aside of these with the outside world from that persons soul. Once this transition takes place, the limitation and separation of human belief and the Eternal no longer are believed in as other humans do without this experience.

"The Divine and the aim of the guardians are for all human souls to reach this mystic enlightenment (experience) for their souls to have eternal rest.

"By this way, that person becomes known as a mystic even though some may cover it over with religious beliefs and ideologies. The mystic experience is the most important and needs to shine forth for all to see and know for themselves.

"In almost every case, when the followers follow the mystic writings and words but have not experienced the Eternal Consciousness for their own, it works out different. What is important about this mystic awareness is not the union of man's souls with the Divine but the parables of events and stories written by man without the Eternal (God) experience.

"What makes it even harder upon one is when religion, faith, and beliefs are set up as the widely accepted authority in a country as a common belief and in their printed words considered to be the Holy Word. One has to set aside all of this and go it alone, cast aside one's fears, insecurity, and all knowledge, and depend upon the truth (God) to be confirmed within one's soul.

"After the truth is one's own, they are without doubt of what the Eternal Divine is. This is true faith, not blind faith and hope. All human souls cannot have this mystic experience at once, yet some have it. It seems to happen at random also.

"You have to be an old soul, it is thought, before one can become of the Divine's awareness, but who is to say?" explained Scott's guardian.

"Then Scott was an old soul?" asked the spirit.

"Who cares? All that matters is that Scott is now one and the same as the Divine Eternal," answered the guardian.

History has shown that all past rulers, religions, morals, etc. worldwide have changed, yet to know the mystic's Eternal Divine has never changed. Within this experience of the Eternal Divine settles the question for the experiencer what the Truth of what God really is. To know this One is the fulfillment of all souls without religion or any other thing or concept upon earth or of the spiritual realm, for this One is beyond these in Absolute Consciousness.

Symbolism

Some years later after Scott's death, there appeared at the village Scott made his home two foreign men. They asked about Scott and were informed that Scott had died but that he left a wife behind.

They requested to be taken to Scott's wife and were taken to her hut after the newcomers were made members of the village where she was resting. Once they entered her hut, they asked her if Scott had left any of his writings behind.

She thought about this for a moment and, getting up off her mat, went to a box and pulled out some old papers and gave them to one of the men. After looking at the papers, one of the men asked the old woman, "Is this all that Scott has, and can we have them?"

The old woman replied, "Those papers are copies of my husband's work. He was one for telling stories to the villagers. The rest of his works were destroyed in a storm, and those are all that is left. Take them if it will help." The woman stated, "Those papers are copies of my husband's notions. He was one for strange thinkers, and no one paid him much attention anyway." What she didn't tell them is that the main body of her husband's work was hidden away where no one could find them because of strangers as these two men before her.

Such men are for gain only, not enlightenment or visions. The two strangers left, and on their way to where they came from, they studied Scott's papers. All they found on those papers were symbolic drawings.

"What the hell is this?" stated one of the men.

"I don't know," answered the other one, perplexed.

"I thought we came all this way to obtain Scott's writings and pay him off so we could sell them to that publisher and make millions," stated the other man.

"Do you think the old woman was lying to us?" asked the young man.

"I don't think so. All islanders are simple-minded," answered the older one.

The old woman knew that when strangers came and asked for things, this is a warning because they want to make much money, and that's no good. By giving out copies of Scott's symbols as she does, she sends out word to any who are dishonest that it's all been a waste of time and a false trail.

Masters, sages, Mystics, Buddhas, and others do the same thing to protect the originals so that they cannot be changed by men who have whatever intentions in their hearts. Changing the originals changes the meaning down the line sooner or later. This is found in all situations.

We could say that symbols are used in all groups and societies. Modern words were developed in groups of symbols as letters. Though there are different letters and symbols around the world, they all have been used to educate their people for communication purposes.

Scott left the world knowing that mankind is still divided on many things, yet he hoped that possibly his works would somehow survive with people who would use them and have an open heart and mind for mankind's advancement of souls. He also knew that even if his writings were not used or destroyed, someday mankind or someone like himself would be born that would develop these truths and write them down and teach them to others.

The Eternal is the same and reveals itself to individuals so that such truths will once again come unto mankind eternally the same yesterday, today, and tomorrow forever.

Once again, the world is full of truths of such insights, yet mankind is prone to the adulterations that blind all eyes and souls to the mystic ways of their philosophies of these truths, which the Absolute's divine essence once experienced brings forth true faith and opens one's spiritual eyes to know this constant always. This constant is the Eternal Divine's absolute truth of eternal rest (God, Tao, etc.)

Afterword on Symbols

Symbols have always been used to represent meanings and are illustrations to humans one to another. Scott used his symbols to convey a story and chapter on important subject matters. Since most people cannot be trusted with Scott's philosophies, they are hidden from most people. These are not meant for them anyway and would do no good for them or the whole world with them. Symbols (illustrations) without the key to explain them are safeguards from society changing the meanings of what Scott finds as truths.

Good intentions more than likely tend to work against the very thing that those intentions were supposed to protect by the followers who have not become enlightened as the mystics and masters have.

The world at large remains in conflict with wars, things as money, material goods, standards or morals, and many other concerns. They tend to keep getting in the way of advancing one's own spiritual growth of the mystic's way of fulfillment with a host of religions or other concepts confusing many in fear, shame, or a host of other words and emotions or actions.

Scott's symbolic illustrations were developed so that his work of the spiritual truths on each subject matter would bring the supreme truth to the ones who read and understand them.

Though it takes generations, there is at least one who comes to this world that has the mystic enlightenment and understands such meanings. That One also is ordained to perform divine sacrifices, and such are between the Eternal and that one individual only, yet there are spiritual guardians that minister unto the one who performs before the Eternal Divine Absolute also.

What has to be done has to be done!

The one who does sacrifice to the Divine in such manners to have Divine Virtue of blessings for the world need not even boast, for boasting is pride, and pride of such is always bad for them. Mystic insights are symbolic and cannot give the full picture of them.

Symbols are used in mystic terms also to represent concepts as the tarot cards or lotus are used to convey meanings of each belief as the cross like the meaning and stands for the belief in Jesus. The mystic has his as the Maya have their drawings to illustrate their meanings. Those who become aware consciously of these truths rest in the Absolute conviction of true faith; this is God and I are the same.

About the Person Scott

The person known as Scott (or David by some) lived with his mother and brothers with different stepfathers. Scott played as any boy. He went to school yet had problems getting good grades. He was more satisfied going out and roaming the neighborhood. As Scott grew up, he viewed life with a simple and single eye, doing what he wanted in life. To him, it was not important to get a good education or a career, let alone to settle down in one place for long or to develop retirement plans or a wife.

Children, by marriage or not, were not to be had in his life so far.

The question would come up again and again within him as to where his place was on earth and who are his people to belong to because his physical family did not seem to be his.

In his travels, it was always the same—he just didn't fit in, nor was any place his home on earth. Through Scott's spiritual experiences and his studies of Eastern philosophies in many other beliefs and writings would bring him into relationship with such people as Lao Tzu, Siddhartha, Jesus, Nichiren, Buddha, Allen Watts, and many more plus his spirit guardians.

Scott could associate himself with them because they also did not really belong to the world or place on earth.

These enlightened ones and Scott's spiritual experiences were akin to each other in which Scott could understand such mystic writings and their meaning and insight.

Scott's poor English and grammar proved to be a blessing instead of a curse because it kept him from reading materials that didn't matter in his quest for the real truth of God (Absolute).

Confinement of any kind went against his free spirit, and he did not sit long in any one place. Prisons proved to be another blessing for Scott because they allowed him to develop his spiritual side in visions, revelations of the Divine, and the mystic experiences plus divine and spiritual rites.

Scott rediscovered his child's clear-sightedness so he could see into men's souls as he saw into his own. His philosophies meant little to others, yet only those who wished, Scott gave answers. Some even thought of him as a fool or liar, and some told him he was promoting the devil's work. Arguing proved nothing, so Scott avoided any that others desired.

Other people would not play fair with him and tried to take advantage of him. Treating others with equality, he was treated as they were his superiors. Scott believed women were his equal and found they used it against him.

He watched a society change from a carefree attitude of children playing everywhere by themselves to one of great concern and fear of harm to them. The children became guarded and watched as inmates are in prison or a socialist dictator's watchful eye.

As Scott developed spiritually, he realized the discovery of the truth, and that truth is the Eternal Divine that is unknown to the world generally.

While Scott lives in the woods with nature, he leaves a world of mankind with its morals, hatred, fear, greed, wealth, progress, and all manner of adulteration in the games people play for real.

Scott saw that the world had some form of religion, belief, or faith, that was organized, and being such caused those followers to be unsatisfied. Some would go to war in the name of their rulers, yet others would defend that same war, claiming justice for all in the name of their god.

Scott found that mankind has a light side as well as a dark side that never comes to rest as this nature alternates within each person. This proves useless to the enlightened ones.

The word God is only another name for man to use to try and understand his Creator's greatness. The Divine is beyond love as mankind defines and understands love.

Scott knows that he has reached the end goal of mankind in being a mystic and has found eternal rest within his soul that he does not have to prove it to anyone. Scott knows that when he dies, his soul (his conscious awareness) will finally become the Eternal Divine at rest, and once this happens, there is no other to advance to (religious heaven, God, dimensions).

There are no more death and ignorance but the Eternal Divine only to Scott that awaits him upon his death and no other.

The Mystic Philosopher

This is what mystic philosopher means:
Mystic: a person who seeks spiritual truths or experiences.

1.   mysterious and awe-inspiring
2.   spiritually allegorical or symbolic
3.   of hidden meaning

Philosopher: a person engaged or learned in philosophy.
Philosophy: the use of reason and argument in seeking truth and knowledge of reality, especially of the causes and nature of things and of the principles governing existence.

1.   metaphysic, logic, rationalism, reason, thinking
2.   viewpoint, ideology, set of values

Comment: This is a person who seeks spiritual truths by experiencing them, and once revealed to that person, they find out and discover the underlying nature and cause of things that support their existence.

Once discovered, one writes, discusses, or argues them, which then are understood. The differences between mystic philosophers and other philosophers is that they do not accept any standard of society in discovering the truth of the spiritual on faith but just seeks the truth by the mystical.

There are two kinds of mystic philosophers. One studies such personal experiences and writes about them, and the second mystic philosopher is the one who does personally experiences such spiritual truths and writes about them.

Mystic philosophy owes its creation to the ones who stepped outside the main stream of society in quest of the truth by design or accident and, once found, leave such spiritual truths for the rest of mankind to be informed about in word or writings.

Mystic philosophies are found in all religions—Christian, LDS (Mormon), Catholic, Buddhist, Hindu, Islam, Taoist, and others.

The Unholy Holy

This is what Unholy Holy means:

Holy: belonging to, devoted to, or empowered by, God; blessed, divine.

Unholy: impious, wicked, dreadful; outrageous, impious, not pious, profane, irreligious, irreverent; sacrilegious, godless, sinful.

Comment: Basically this is a person viewed by others or society as not being as they are to religious authority and beliefs. This is a person outside religious beliefs and does not conform to that standard.

The mystic is viewed by religious morals as being unholy yet the mystic experience of God or the Divine itself is a holy matter—that is they are empowered and blessed by the Divine Absolute.

Once upon a time, it was believed that a holy man lived on an island, so a young couple made up their minds to travel and see him. After the couple was taken to the island, they were shown an old man who appeared not to be native to the region.

The young man of the couple walked up to this old man and introduced themselves. The young woman of this couple asked the old man if he was the holy man that they had come to see.

The old one turned away from them for a moment then faced them, saying, "What have you come here to see?"

"We've come to talk to a holy man we heard about in our country," answered the young man.

"Why?" asked the old one.

"Because we heard that he had the answer to God," replied the woman.

"This is your answer: 'I AM GOD,'" returned the old one.

"What! How can you be God? You're just like us with flesh and blood in a physical body, and besides, you don't look holy to me. I understand that God is all holy and man is unholy and that the two are different," replied the young man.

The old man explained to the couple, "Societies of religious authorities and nonreligious ones have been led to believe and have accepted that the Divine or what you call God is something other than what it really is. People on their death beds believe that when they pass on that they will go to either a heaven, hell, or what have you to be with their God. Sit down and have a native drink and excuse my impoliteness, but we do not get many visitors here on this island," instructed the old one.

As the young couple sat on the floor, they were given a drink by an old native woman.

"We heard also that there was a mystic here," stated the young man.

The old man laughed and shook his head and answered, saying, "First things first. There has been a misunderstanding. Whoever told you of such things always makes a big deal out of more than what it really is. Once someone is claimed to be holy, then this concept has already been misunderstood by the masses."

The old man asked the couple, "Do you see me with a halo over my head or doing supernatural things?"

"No," replied the young man.

"Then I must not be holy, and since I'm not holy, I must be unholy. A holy man does not have the vices of man as I do in smoking tobacco, drinking alcohol, or having sex. I know that I'm of the Divine Eternal Soul, though my physical body dies. After my death I merge with the Divine Eternal Soul as it is without any heaven to go to but am the pure essence of the Divine, not to a heaven or any such place as others would have us believe. Even using the word God is misleading. Let's use other words than God and use Eternal or Divine instead or Absolute. The Eternal does not need a human image, but man makes the Eternal into the human form so man can believe in his higher self.

"People who accept that the Eternal (God) has a human form already created a separation between themselves and God (the Eternal Divine). Mankind perceives their God as in relationship to themselves. That is that their God has a father image with offspring, and if that offspring (Child) misbehaves or doesn't worship or do what the first son or prophet tells them to do, then the offspring will get punished. This is about the same as earthly parents are and do with their own children. The concept and belief is easy to understand by humans. The human soul then does not have a God Mother, only a God Father in their belief. This concept is of the Christian, Hebrew, and Islam religions, and other beliefs. Other faiths and beliefs see their spirit guides in human form also.

"I'm not holy or a saint, for I am only a man who has experienced the eternal consciousness, which is enlightenment of the Divine (God). My consciousness and the Divine's consciousness merge into the One! When a person experiences this awareness, that person is known as a mystic. This experience only lasts for an instant, and then one's awareness comes back to its normal self again, but as it were charged up in one's soul," explained the old mystic.

"If I wish to experience this mystic consciousness, then how do I go about it?" asked the young man.

The old man answered him, saying, "Pray for the truth to be revealed to you with an open heart in honesty, and reject all religious beliefs and faiths. Seek your own quest in this, and be ready to even give up your own life and soul to this truth (God). If it is for you to perceive this revelation, enlightenment of the Eternal Divine experience, then it will be revealed to you. If it is not revealed to you, then there may be other reasons why it does not happen sooner or later. Even mystics do not understand why everyone does not have this experience in their lifetime. It may have something to do with their soul's fate within that lifetime. The Creative Force (Eternal Divine), as well as the spirits, reveals only certain things to the mystic of their life and a bit of other things. So it is up to each individual to seek their own," explained the mystic to the couple.

After all was said, the young couple bid their farewell and left the island. The old man's wife came to him and asked, "Scott, do you think that the young couple really believed you and will follow your advice?"

"Who knows, maybe, but at least they found out about the holy man thing that I wasn't such a misconception. Hopefully, this will get them to dispel many ideas about what they heard about me from others. When any society makes or creates anything holy and develops a religion around it, they have already planted the seeds of conflict and unrest, which this misinformation is believed in as the Holy Word," stated her husband.

By the time the sun was setting, Scott gave his wife a loving hug and kiss, then he told her that he loved her and their daughter.

As night came, they went to their hut and slept soundly.

Is a mystic holy then? He does not see himself as holy, nor should anyone else. To place anyone upon a pedestal as being holy or sinful only serves the vanity of others that do not know nor have experienced such enlightenment for themselves.

The mystic is a lowly humble soul in innocence as a child and flows to the Divine as a river flows to the sea and beyond being holy or sinful yet has true faith, realizing that the Divine Eternal and their souls consciousness are the SAME ONE!

Others that only believe that God comes to their religious belief as the only true one do not know the workings of primal virtue that is pure of spirit very well or at all, nor of the Divine Absolute.

Eternal Rest

"Those who do not become aware of the mystic experience will not find eternal rest."

The Eternal is that state of being eternally at rest and never changing. This is known as the truth, because it is always the same and constant.

When the mystic experiences this state of eternal rest, his soul has merged with the Eternal Divine, and they are one and the same Absolute. When this experience takes place afterward, that individual's doubts disappear about what the truth is.

This is the supreme goal of mankind, and once this happens, there is no need to try to confirm one's belief in any other thing or faith because there isn't any other. All others fall short of this mystic experience and comes short of being at rest, and being eternally at one with the One is eternally restful.

Is this not being fulfilled? Yes!

Christ, Buddha, Siddhartha, Lao Tzu, Nichiren, the mystic, and others all knew this and are fulfilled within this same eternal restfulness. Our consciousness tells the story to each individual's fate and so to the mystics.

The Earth Passes

After Scott died, the world continued to be at war and in conflict in which millions of people died. The earth's weather changed, and millions more died. Mankind developed space travel and moved to other planets to colonize them. Children were born, and all were well again for the settlements. The old earth could not support human life anymore, and the world became a rock in space and, as they say, died.

Sometime later, on a small planet, an infant man-child was born with a head of white hair, and he grew up to become a mystic to bless mankind. He would experience revelations of the eternal knowledge to reveal to mankind, yet once again, after his death, he would be misunderstood by his followers of his knowledge.

Once again, this proves that the Eternal is needed for the souls of human beings as it has been for centuries and eons. If other life-forms as advance as human beings are in the universe, they too may have souls as mankind has, which the Eternal Divine will make its presence known to them as it has with all the mystics and enlightened ones on earth. The Absolute then gathers its other souls-self until it is whole again.

The Illustrated Mystic

The illustrated mystic can be found as a lone individual wearing a hooded long monks robe standing atop the high snowcapped peak. He holds a staff with one hand and a lantern in the other with a star in it. He looks down upon the valley below. All around him is a gray mist.

This illustration conveys the meaning of what it means when one has become an enlightened individual to the Eternal Divine. They hold the eternal divine light within them, and the rest of the world is a mist, illusion, and dream-state gray mist.

He has advanced to the highest state of mankind as one would reach the high mountain peaks. He is alone, for he alone has the Eternal Divine's truth with his soul, and it shines forth to all others as a shining beacon for their guidance.

To the rest of the world, they are in the bright sunlight of this physical world of the illustrated mystic's gray mist, illusion, or dream state. They are asleep, but the mystic is fully awake unto the Eternal Divine's essence in absolute perfection.

This is a problem with many faiths; they just haven't set their goals high enough beyond their god's image, shape, and form onto becoming God's (Absolute) consciousness (essence) themselves.

Trial of the Soul

Some individuals are called by the Divine to experience what is known as the trial of the soul. This trial separates the wheat from the chaff as it were—that is, it extinguishes the adulteration within that person's soul while in the physical world.

This trial is a test of spiritual fire by sacrifice and suffering. One's soul and spirit are purified of contamination and pollution of the spiritual and physical realms until all that remains is the purified, washed, or cleansed heart and soul.

This purified soul then is able to stand before the Divine Creator so as to be judged of its fitness for the divine purpose of blessings of divine virtue unto other souls on earth.

The story of Scott is written to explain that the Divine reveals itself in an unorthodox way to individuals, whether they are religious or not. In most cases, it is the individualist who seeks the truth about the Eternal Divine (God), not the other way around. Once the door is opened, then the Divine is revealed, and that person is set free, sanctified, fulfilled, and complete.

If the Divine depends upon a particular religious faith of any established order or situation before it is allowed to reveal itself to those worshipers, it would be quite foolish and misleading, plus it would be disgraceful to others.

The true enlightened of the Divine, who knows it personally, questions not the experience and has absolutely no doubts about the Divine Eternal Absolute. This individual then is known as the illustrated mystic.

Mankind alone without this Divine experience is left to make or develop morals and is not the guiding lantern of the Illustrated One or of the Absolute's aim.

The trial of the soul of man is needed for the divine blessings of virtue, though the mystic experience can happen without this trail and purification.

Many parts of the ancient and modern world from pre-Christian, Christian, Taoist, Buddhist, etc., all have experienced such trial of the soul and mystic enlightenment as the mystic has. It is the same with all of them of the Divine Eternal and such primal virtue for the blessings of souls.

Mankind within their separate faiths seem not to get the point that they all are drawing from the same source eternally and spiritually—some to heaven, some to angelic beings, and some to the source itself, as they believe. The mystic knows this source is the Absolute.

Illustrations

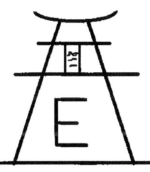

This is the symbol used for a gateway, Torii in Japanese.

This gateway also has many meanings, yet it is also the gateway to God or Enlightenment (Eternal Divine), Mystic, Absolute. These symbols are found in the Orient and placed where it is believed such gateway shows what is held as the best of nature, God, spirits, and man, making God visible on earth.

This gateway also can be used by the enlightened or mystic as these individuals are also the gateway to the Eternal Divine (God) manifested within.

The *E* in this illustration stands for Eternal within.

Lao Tzu's Way (Tao Te Ching).

The *I Ching*'s Hexagram 1, the Creative. The lines deal with the mystical dragon, the sage, mystics, superior man, etc.

Within mystic rites, one as the mediator serves as the gateway between mankind (humans) and the Divine and spirits as a go-between as it were as a gateway to the Absolute of the beyond.

Each individual is responsible for their own enlightenment of the Absolute.

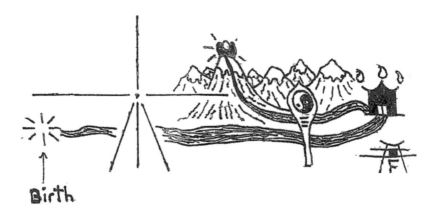

Birth

This illustration is the representation of a mystic's life (Scott).

This shows the road of life from birth unto death and the means by which some men know the Eternal Divine and other such insights to the Utmost.

At the end of their physical lives, they merge at the top of the mountains to become divine (hermit), the Absolute.

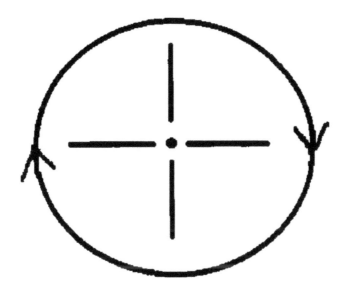

The circle with these arrows show it is ever moving. It is the sign of what I use to illustrate the enlightenment of man to the Divine. The center represents the ever-living or ever-being of the Divine that all mystics experience enclosed within their personal soul.

Since this experience of the Divine Eternal cannot be put in words nor correctly drawn or shown in its reality, this illustration is a dim attempt to express it.

The only way for anyone to truly know the Divine is by a personal awareness in their consciousness of the Absolute. Once this happens, they will totally understand and know of the Divine Eternal, Tao, God, Enlightenment, Jesus, Buddha, Siddhartha, Lao Tzu, Nichiren, Sage, Mystic, etc., all know this and more.

Before mystic rites are performed, the mystic mediator has to confront the Divine Eternal in consciousness and request for its approval to perform them for mankind.

This brings about the development of primal virtue (spiritually) from the Divine (Tao), or some would say Holy Ghost.

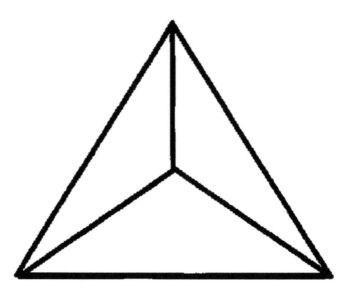

Triangle has three sides, and so does the Trinity of mankind of body, mind, and soul. In this case in our triangle, all points lead inward and meet in the center to form another three-sided illusion. This gives the illusion of another dimension as one would view a pyramid from above.

This perception sets one's mind to see what isn't there on paper yet one can mentally form a dimension of the fourth. This man's makeup of a fourth factor is added in perceiving beyond the soul to the super consciousness or the God-Self at the center, Divine realized.

We think in three dimensions, but we can experience the fourth dimension in our souls. Enlightenment of the Divine is the ultimate dimension unity in the fourth. These three dimensions are tied in with the fourth as a working whole and, in this way, brings one unto the fulfillment of one's soul in emergence with the Divine Eternal, quest ended and eternal rest absolute!

The Absolute Divine's aim is the individual's quest to seek it, and once experienced, it claims its own upon their passing.

9

The number 9 is for the completion of the single numbers, which is also the number of the mystic and enlightened ones.

These then have completed all and have found the Eternal Divine, which is the final goal of mankind. The fulfillment of all things comes to the physical world and on the spiritual realm or dimension of cycles and numbers.

We could say that zero (0) is also the illustration of the Eternal, and the zero is without end and timeless.

Numerology's nine (9) stands for completion. Tarot cards' nine (9) of the major cards stands for the hermit enlightenment, mystic, and so on.

It takes nine months from conception to birth of human babies. It takes nine months from Divine consent and the beginning of the mystic rites unto their end. It takes some nine years from the impregnation of the would-be mystic mediator with the primal seed of virtue (lotus) until its fruition to bless mankind spiritually, but some ten months to end this process fully with mystic rites to heal him, some believe. Does not this means that the mystic within these matters is the cosmic womb for the embryo of the Absolute's aim and begotten? Yes!

Infinity, or eternity, is another form used by man.

Infinity is also like the mystic, who knows no bounds of the spirit.

Infinity also means infinite, that is being limitless or endless and inexhaustible as the Divine is once one becomes aware of the Divine Eternal Absolute.

So too has the mystic and the enlightened of the Eternal Divine experienced the infinite and its essence without end.

Everlasting blessings for others in primal virtue of the unfathomable vast unknown to most.

Last Word

The near-death experience (NDE) it would seem is a form people experience that brings testimony of the spiritual dimension that throws light upon another side of our souls. The seer, whether mystic or not, becomes aware by direct participation of the spiritual personages, develops direct faith in such, and tends to cause one to lose the fear of death. Both mystic and the "near-death experience" person goes a long way to change long-held beliefs that religions have of what happens after one dies (pass on).

As in times past, it changes from one advanced society to another, so mankind's concepts and insights change once again. If revelations of the Bible is set in stone, then all manner of spiritual insights as enlightenments, Buddha, and near-death experience have no room as in Revelation's heaven. Are these experiences then of Satan? I think *not*.

This present volume shows another side of spiritualness, and if I am wrong and fooled, then I have received my reward already, but so has all the others. If I am right, then mankind *is* advancing according to a higher spiritual being and soul's growth and advance beyond the old long-held dogmas of religions, society, and beliefs.

Note: Blessings

Down through written history, we have testament to declare spiritu-ally that inspires followers of many such religions and faiths that have been blessed by their membership and belief by the Creative Force, God, Tao, or the spiritual realm.

I have been blessed by Mormons, Shoshu Buddhists, guardian spirits, the Spirit, the mystic's spirit mother, the Tao, the Absolute, etc.

The Universal Life Church philosophy is one that believes that we are all spiritually inspired, but different societies tend to separate themselves from each other with their different religions.

I tend to understand this, and I say that we all shall pass on to obtain our just reward upon our own faith. Sound conflictive, not really. People may change religions and bear witness of it, yet all believers believe in a higher force than themselves, and so shall it be.

What makes anyone believe that theirs is the only one that brings blessings from the Utmost upon this physical realm? If so then they are of closed minds and truth is hidden from them! There is but one Creator of all souls, but each receives God's truth in their own way.

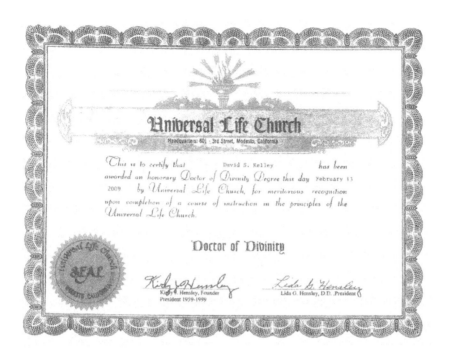

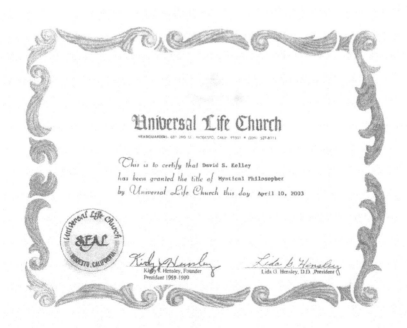

About the Author

David Scott Kelley, also known as Scott, was born with a full head of white hair. He had his first mystic experience at the age of twenty-three or so while in prison. He became a Shoshu Buddhist at about twenty-eight and, some years later, experienced spiritual ministries from the spiritual realm for ten months. Kelley received his mystic philosopher certification from the Universal Life Church in 2003 and doctor of divinity on February 13, 2009. Kelley studied eastern philosophies to further his knowledge and help him in his spiritual endeavors with the supernatural forces and spiritual plain. Kelley continues to write about such spiritual meaning and enlightenments. He now is known as a mystic and has given up Shoshu Buddhism to advance upon the mountain peaks and become what is known as the Hermit to write and await his emergence of eternal rest of the Eternal Divine. In the meantime, Kelley writes and prepares to study "pristine simplicity" way of life of primitive peoples of the world. Kelley's other experiences came from LDS (Mormons), Tibetan, and Buddhist spiritual insights spiritually, spiritual beings, God, etc., which advanced his spiritual growth of his soul.

CPSIA information can be obtained
at www.ICGtesting.com
Printed in the USA
FFHW021950240419
51989833-57404FF